The Pyramid Builders

By Heather Hammonds

Illustrations by Christen Stewart

Contents

Title	Text Type	Pages
The Great Pyramid of Giza	Information Report	2–9
Building the Great Pyramid	Recount	10–16

The Great Pyramid of Giza

The Great Pyramid of Giza is in Egypt. It was built more than 4500 years ago. Thousands of workers from villages and towns all over Egypt built the pyramid.

Many of the workers who built the pyramid lived beside it during its construction. Supervisors and other permanent workers lived in a nearby town with their families. It is believed there were about 5000 permanent workers at the pyramid.

Temporary workers travelled to Giza to work on the pyramid for three or four months. They lived in a camp beside the main town. Around 20 000 workers lived in the camp.

After they had finished working on the pyramid they returned to their villages and towns.

excavations near the pyramids at Giza

Thousands of workers put these stones in place.

It took 20 years to construct the Great Pyramid of Giza. There were many different jobs to be done.

Some workers helped put the massive stones in place. Other workers skilfully made tools, or built ramps for the stones.

bronze and wooden tools

There were factories near the workers' town and camp. Some factories manufactured goods such as metal tools. Others made bread or other foods, or provided meat for the workers.

Pyramid workers were paid their wages in beer and loaves of bread. These could be swapped for other food and goods the workers needed, such as clothing.

making bread

Scientists continue to discover more and more about the Great Pyramid of Giza. They have examined the remains of the workers' camp and town, and the writing and pictures on walls, in order to learn about its amazing history.

The Great Pyramid of Giza is still standing today.

Building the Great Pyramid

Dear Sister,

A scribe has written this for me to let you know I arrived safely at the building site of the Great Pyramid last week.

The pyramid is an amazing sight. It will be enormous when it is completed.

My supervisor told me I will work here for four months.

A place in the temporary workers' camp was found for me and I have settled in well. The camp is beside the main workers' town.

Yesterday I walked through the town on my way to work, as I do each day.

Senior and permanent workers live there in mudbrick houses and I walked past my supervisor's house, which is larger than many of the others.

When I arrived here I was made part of a team of construction workers. We are called "The Friends of the King".

Yesterday our team helped put a large stone block in position on the pyramid wall. It was very hot, hard work.

After work, we were paid our weekly wages in food and drink. My wages were ten loaves of bread and a measure of beer.

Walking back through the town, I collected my bread from the bakery and beer from the brewery. All the workers are able to exchange their bread and beer for other goods, so I got some meat for my dinner.

I returned to my camp site, where many thousands of workers are staying.

It was a hard day's work and I was very tired, but I am glad that I volunteered to work on the Great Pyramid.

From,

Your brother